This book belongs to

....

Quarto is the authority on a wide range of topics.

Quarto educates, entertains and enriches the lives of our readers—enthusiasts and lovers of hands-on living.

www.quartoknows.com

© 2018 Quarto Publishing plc

First published in 2018 by QED Publishing,
an imprint of The Quarto Group.
The Old Brewery, 6 Blundell Street,
London N7 9BH, United Kingdom.
T (0)20 7700 6700 F (0)20 7700 8066
www.QuartoKnows.com

A catalogue record for this book is available from the
British Library.

ISBN 978-1-78493-924-3

Based on the original story by Robert Dunn
Author of adapted text: Katie Woolley
Series Editor: Joyce Bentley
Series Designer: Sarah Peden

Manufactured in Dongguan, China TL102017

9 8 7 6 5 4 3 2 1

MIX
Paper from
responsible sources
FSC® C104723

Reading
Gems

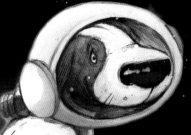

Moon
Dog

Patch liked to play chase
in the garden.

He liked to sleep on the bed.

He liked to eat
his tea.

Patch got in lots of trouble.

But Patch wanted to go to the
moon most of all.

One day Patch saw a big rocket in the garden.

Patch wanted to go in the rocket.

He saw lots of buttons. Patch sat on a big button.

Blast off! The rocket went up and up.

Patch was in trouble.

Patch could not stop the rocket.

Bump went the rocket and bump went Patch.

The rocket landed on the moon!
Patch got out to play.

Patch saw the moon dogs.
He played chase.

But Patch wanted to go home.

Patch bounced off the moon.

Blast off!

Down, down, down he fell.

Patch fell faster and faster!
He could not stop.

Patch landed in his bed.

Patch liked the moon but he liked home most of all.

Story Words

bed

blast off

button

eat

moon

moon dog

Patch

rocket

sat

tea

trouble

Let's Talk About Moon Dog

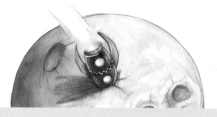

Look carefully at the book cover.

Where is Patch?

What is he wearing?

Having read the story, how do you think Patch feels about being on the moon?

Have a look at the pictures on pages 5 and 6.

What is Patch doing in each one?

Does Patch look happy in all the pictures?

Space is a big place!

Would you like to go into space one day?

How would you get there?

What would you take with you?

Patch is happy to be home at the end of the story.

Why do you think this is?

What do you think he missed while he was on the moon?

What things would you miss?

If you found a new planet, what would you call it?

What would it look like and who do you think might live there?

Fun and Games

Look at the pictures. What are they?
What letter sound does each word begin with?
Follow the trails to see if you were right!

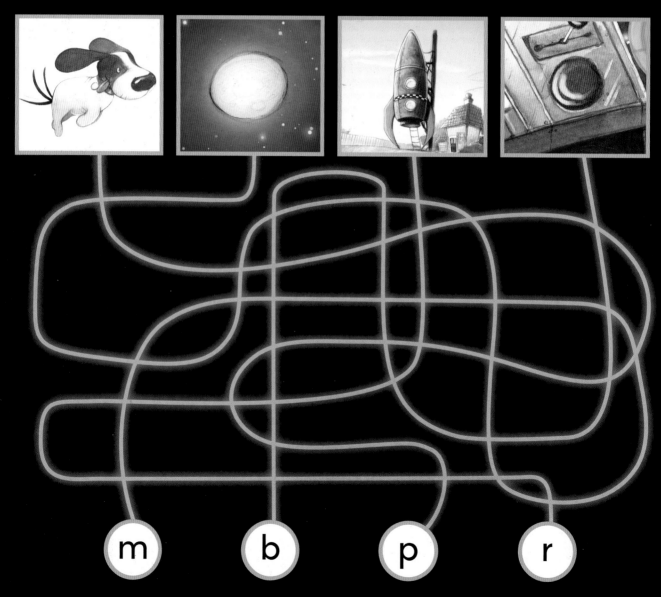

Can you match the words to the pictures?

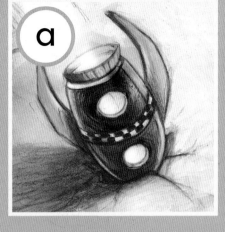

bed

blast off

down, down, down

landed

Your Turn

Now that you have read the story,
have a go at telling it in your own words.
Use the pictures below to help you.

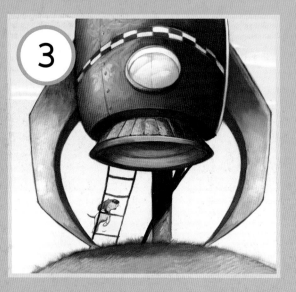

GET TO KNOW READING GEMS

Reading Gems is a series of books that has been written for children who are learning to read. The books have been created in consultation with a literacy specialist.

The books fit into four levels, with each level getting more challenging as a child's confidence and reading ability grows. The simple text and fun illustrations provide gradual, structured practice of reading. Most importantly, these books are good stories that are fun to read!

Level 1 is for children who are taking their first steps into reading. Story themes and subjects are familiar to young children, and there is lots of repetition to build reading confidence.

Level 2 is for children who have taken their first reading steps and are becoming readers. Story themes are still familiar but sentences are a bit longer, as children begin to tackle more challenging vocabulary.

Level 3 is for children who are developing as readers. Stories and subjects are varied, and more descriptive words are introduced.

Level 4 is for readers who are rapidly growing in reading confidence and independence. There is less repetition on the page, broader themes are explored and plot lines straddle multiple pages.

Moon Dog follows Patch as he has his very own space adventure. It explores themes of play, misadventure and the importance of home.

Level 2

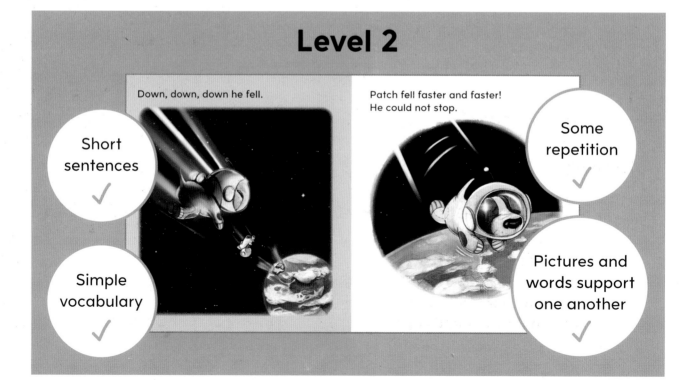

Down, down, down he fell.

Patch fell faster and faster! He could not stop.

Short sentences ✓

Simple vocabulary ✓

Some repetition ✓

Pictures and words support one another ✓